I CAN DO HARD THINGS

MINDFUL AFFIRMATIONS FOR KIDS

Gabi Garcia

Illustrated by **Charity Russell**

I don't always feel brave, confident, or strong. Sometimes it seems easier to follow others along.

I get so many messages about how I should be.

Pulled in different directions, I feel wobbly!

When this happens, I listen for that quiet voice inside. When I pay attention, that voice is my guide.

I connect with the love and strength it brings. It helps me remember: I can do hard things.

I can be a friend to myself.

I can feel all my feelings.

I can ask for help.

I can try again, rather than give up.

I can speak up when it would
be easier to stay quiet.

I can say no, even to my friends.

I can apologize.

I can forgive.

I can listen to understand different points of view.

I can care for my community.

I can choose kindness.

I can share my gifts with the world.

I can be myself.

Hard things can be about what we think,
feel, say, or do.

What's hard for me may not be hard for you.

You are you, and I am me.

We walk through the world differently.

Trusting my voice helps me find my way.

I grow braver and stronger every day.

The tough stuff I
face is all my
own.

But I can also remember I'm not alone.

I'm ready for the hard things I have to do.

And please remember, so are you!

MINDFUL AFFIRMATIONS

To be **mindful** is to be aware of what is happening right now. An **affirmation** is a short phrase or statement about yourself that is supportive, helpful or motivating to you in some way.

Mindful affirmations connect you with what you need to hear. Find one for yourself!

1. Choose an affirmation that you connect with from the book, or come up with your own.

2. Take a few deep breaths. Repeat it silently to yourself. Pay attention to physical sensations (energized, strong, tingly, calm, relaxed, etc.) and notice how saying your affirmation makes you feel (loving, brave, proud, curious, excited, peaceful, etc.).

3. Think about how this affirmation is supportive or helpful to you. If it isn't helpful or supportive, choose another one.

4. Write your affirmation down. Place it somewhere that you'll see it and repeat it to yourself.

What you say to yourself matters! Mindful affirmations become your inner voice, which supports you in doing hard things-- whatever they may be for you.

Dedicated to children doing hard things every day.

skinned knee
publishing
902 Gardner Rd. No. 4
Austin, Texas 78721

Publisher's Cataloging-in-Publication data
Names: Garcia, Gabi, author. | Russell, Charity, illustrator.
Title: I can do hard things : mindful affirmations for kids / Gabi Garcia ; illustrated by Charity Russell.
Description: Austin, TX: Skinned Knee Publishing, 2018.
Identifiers: ISBN 978-1-949633-00-9 (Hardcover) | 978-0-9989580-8-8 (pbk.) |978-0-9989580-9-5 (ebook)
Summary: Introduces children to the practice of listening to their quiet voice inside and using mindful affirmations for support when navigating hard situations when they arise.
Subjects: LCSH Meditation for children. | Awareness--Juvenile literature. | Emotions in children--Juvenile literature. | Self-esteem--Juvenile literature. | Conduct of life. | JUVENILE NONFICTION / Body, Mind & Spirit. | JUVENILE NONFICTION / Health & Daily Living / General. | JUVENILE NONFICTION / Health & Daily Living / Daily Activities.
Classification: LCC BF637.M4 .G36 2018 | DDC 158.1/28--dc23

Gabi Garcia is a mama, licensed professional counselor and picture book author. She spent the last 20 years working with children as a school counselor. Gabi writes books that support parents, educators and caregivers in nurturing mindful, socially and emotionally aware children. She lives with her family in Austin, Texas

Visit gabigarciabooks.com for FREE downloadable resorces that accompany this book.

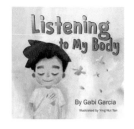

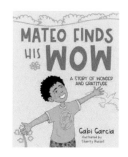

OTHER BOOKS BY GABI GARCIA
ALL TITLES AVAILABLE IN SPANISH

Charity Russell lives with her husband and two children in Bristol. She attended Falmouth University College where she obtained a Bachelors degree in Illustration and Design, followed a few years later by a Master degree from the University of Sunderland.

You can see her work and contact her through her website charityrussell.com.

Made in the USA
Middletown, DE
16 November 2021